when's my birthday?

Julie
Fogliano

Christian
Robinson

WALKER BOOKS
AND SUBSIDIARIES
LONDON • BOSTON • SYDNEY • AUCKLAND

when's my birthday?
where's my birthday?
how many days until
my birthday?

will my birthday be on tuesday?
will my birthday be tomorrow?
will my birthday be in winter?

will my birthday be in spring?

will my birthday have some singing?
will we sing so happy happy?
will we dance around and round?
will we jump and jump and jump?

ny days until

nday?

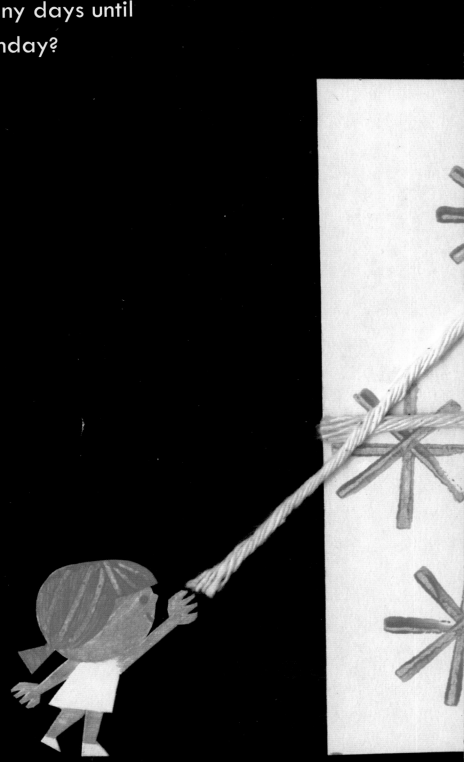

i'd like a pony
for my birthday
and a necklace
for my birthday.

i'd like a
chicken for
my birthday.

i'd like a ball
to bounce
and bounce.

i'd like a big cake on my birthday
with lots of chocolate on my birthday
and lots of candles on my birthday
1, 2, 3, 4, 5, and 6!

i'd like some wishes on my birthday.
i'd like some kisses on my birthday.
i'd like some berries on my birthday
and tiny sandwiches with soup.

and you're invited
to my birthday.

and she's invited
to my birthday.

and he's invited
to my birthday.

and you and
you and you.

and you can wear your fancy dresses
or you can wear your fuzzy slippers
or you can wear a hat with feathers
or a helmet with a cape.

if it ever is my birthday...
will it never be my birthday?
is it almost happy birthday?
happy happy day to me!

when's my birthday?
where's my birthday?
how many days until
my birthday?

In the morning it's my birthday!
I'm not sleeping till my birthday.
I'm just waiting till my birthday.
I'm just yawning till my birthday.
I'm just dreaming of my bluuuurfday.
Happy snore and snore to me!

it's the daytime!
here's my birthday!
happy happy!
hee! hee! hee!
time for cakey
wakey wakey

happy happy day to me!

When's Your Birthday?

January 1 2 3 4

February

March 8 9 10

April

May 14 15

June

July

August 19 20 21

September

October 24 25

November 29 30 31

December

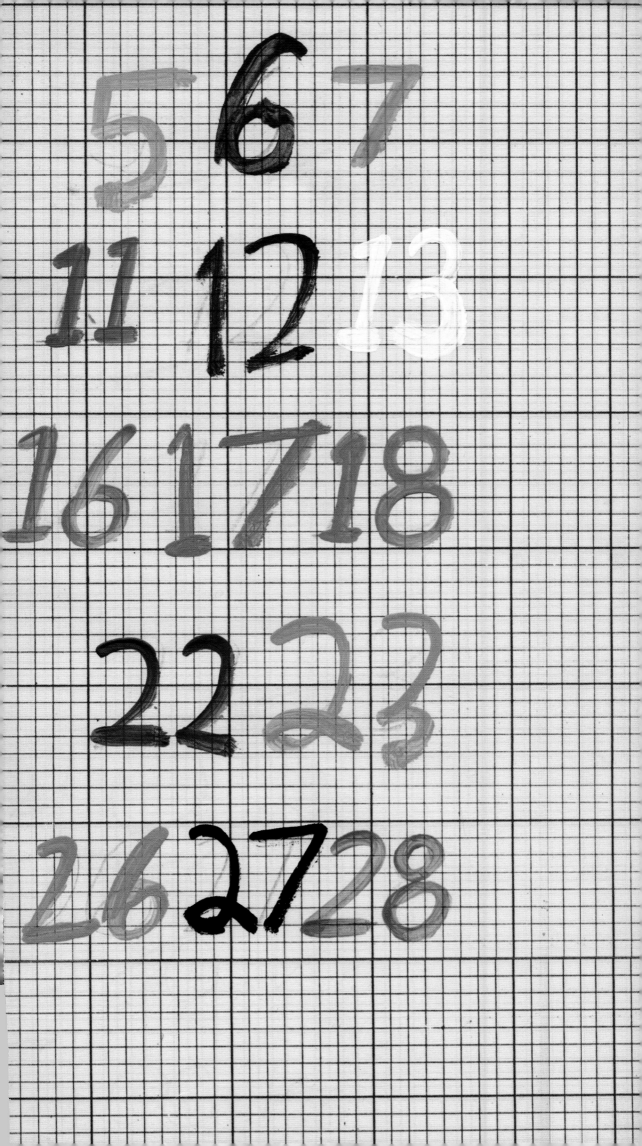